Playing with

Story by Carmel Reilly

Illustrations by Jenny Mountstephen

Rigby

A Harcourt Achieve Imprint

www.Rigby.com
1-800-531-5015

2

Mom and Tessa and Alice
went to the park.

"We can play hide and seek,"
Tessa said to Mom and Alice.
"You run away and hide,
and I will come to find you."

Tessa saw Milly,
the new girl from school.

She saw Milly
getting out of the car
with her dad.

"Hello, Milly," said Tessa.

"Come and play hide and seek

with us."

"Thank you, Tessa," said Milly.

"I can't play hide and seek.

I can walk, but I can't run fast

like you."

"**I** will play with you," said Tessa.

"Will you?" said Milly.

"Yes, we can play on the swings,"
said Tessa.

"I love playing on the swings,"
said Milly.

Tessa said to her mother,
"Can I play on the swings
with Milly?"

"Can I please play, too?"
said Alice.

"Yes," said Mom, "go and play."

"I love coming here," said Milly.

"We love it, too," said Tessa.